A Cote of Many Colors

Janette Oke's Animal Friends

JANETTE OKE'S

Animal Friends

A Cote of Many Colors

Illustrated by Nancy Munger

BETHANY BACKYARD®

A Cote of Many Colors
Revised, full-color edition 2001
Copyright © 1987, 2001
Janette Oke

Illustrations by Nancy Munger
Design by Jennifer Parker

Published by Bethany House Publishers
A Ministry of Bethany Fellowship International
11400 Hampshire Avenue South
Minneapolis, Minnesota 55438
www.bethanyhouse.com

Printed in China

Library of Congress Cataloging-in-Publication Data

Oke, Janette, 1935-
  A cote of many colors / by Janette Oke; illustrated by Nancy Munger.— Rev. full-color ed.
     p. cm. — (Janette Oke's animal friends)
Summary: When their caretaker is hospitalized, Blue Boy and the other homing pigeons receive food, water, and excellent care from two young boys who love pets.
  ISBN 0-7642-2459-X (pbk.)
  [1. Homing pigeons—Juvenile fiction. 2. Homing pigeons—Fiction. 3. Pigeons—Fiction. 4. Pets—Fiction.] I. Munger, Nancy, ill. II. Title.
  PZ10.3 O338 Co 2001
  [Fic]—dc21

                               2001001251

ISBN 0-7642-2459-X

Dedicated with love and appreciation
to "fancier" Neil Neufeld,
my former pastor and long-time friend,
and in memory of his dear wife, Gladys.

JANETTE OKE was born in Champion, Alberta, during the depression years, to a Canadian prairie farmer and his wife. She is a graduate of Mountain View Bible College in Didsbury, Alberta, where she met her husband, Edward. Both Janette and Edward have been active in their local church as Sunday school teachers and board members. The Okes have four grown children and several grandchildren and make their home near Calgary, Alberta.

CHAPTER
One

Let me introduce myself. My name is Blue Boy, and I am a homing pigeon. You might think I'm like any other pigeon. But I'm not. I'm a special bird just for racing. I've even won awards for the way I can fly.

Homing pigeons are trained to fly a very long way, as much as six hundred miles! We can go great distances. But what makes us special is that we always find our way home. We used to carry messages in a special pouch. That's how people who lived far away from each other could send letters back and forth. These days, our owners like to train us to be the fastest. We get together with other pigeons to race.

But that's not why I'm telling my story right now. You see, something very special happened to me and my owner a while ago. I want to tell you about it.

My owner's name was Mr. Faraday. He loved his pigeons. He had lots of us, and we lived in a special birdhouse, called a loft, in Mr. Faraday's backyard. He took great care of us, making sure we had just the right food and water. And he trained us to fly several miles and return home, as fast as we could.

But what Mr. Faraday did not love was

other people, especially children. His birds were the only thing that mattered to him. So even though he had been very happy raising us birds, the rest of his life was pretty lonely.

This is the story of how Mr. Faraday's life was completely changed, and how I got to be one of the luckiest homing pigeons in the entire world.

CHAPTER
Two

Mr. Faraday was a gruff, grouchy old man. And it was too bad he didn't like children, because two of the friendliest boys I'd ever met lived just next door. The boys liked to lean over the fence and watch Mr. Faraday care for us birds.

It was easy to see that Mark and Timmie loved us pigeons. But then, Mark and Timmie also loved cats—and dogs. They loved ponies and lambs and hamsters and rabbits. But Mark and Timmie had no pets—not one. And Mr. Faraday was the reason.

The house where Mark and Timmie lived was rented from Mr. Faraday. Mr. Faraday didn't like cats—they chased birds.

And he didn't like dogs—they barked and scared his flock. So he told the boys absolutely no pets allowed.

It wasn't a very fancy house, but there was plenty of fresh air and room to run, and a big garden spot. There were even trees to climb. Mark and Timmie could have been very happy where they lived, had it not been for gruff Mr. Faraday and his strict rules. "No pets," he said. And he stressed it over and over to the boys' mother. "Any pets and you are out, no second chances."

So Mark and Timmie could only crowd to the fence that separated the yards and eagerly watch the pigeons.

C H A P T E R
Three

One morning that summer, I woke up and knew something was wrong. The other birds in my flock were flapping their wings and pacing around.

"Where is he, anyway?" someone asked.

A plump, blue-gray bird tapped his foot and scowled at the sun high in the sky. "He has never been late before," he said.

"No—and there's a reason for it now," shot back another bird. "It's way, way past breakfast. He must know we're starving."

I looked down at our feeding trough and saw it was empty. *How strange*, I thought to myself. *Mr. Faraday is never late giving us our meals. I wonder what happened?*

I climbed up to the top of our loft to get a good look at the small yellow house Mr. Faraday lived in. It didn't look like anyone was moving about in there.

The pigeons below me shifted around uneasily. The soft, happy cooing that usually came in the morning had stopped. Instead, the voices now sounded mad—worried. Where was the man with our breakfast?

"Do you see anything, Blue Boy?" asked several of the older pigeons almost in unison.

"Nothing," I told them. "No one is stirring. There is no sign of Mr. Faraday anywhere."

My stomach rumbled loudly. *Where is the man? Where is breakfast?*

Great coos of concern rang out from the loft. If Mr. Faraday didn't come out to feed us, what would happen to us all?

CHAPTER
Four

I caught a flash of movement at the fence. It was Mark and Timmie. The boys were there as usual, waiting to watch Mr. Faraday feed the birds. But even to the young children, it was obvious something was wrong. I could just hear what they were saying.

"What's wrong with them?" Timmie whispered.

"I don't know," responded his older brother. "But something sure is bothering them."

"Do you see any cats?" Timmie asked.

Mark studied the backyard carefully before answering. "Nothing," he said. "Not a movement anywhere."

There was silence for a moment. Both boys were thinking. Timmie voiced their thoughts.

"Do you see Mr. Faraday?"

"No," said Mark, shaking his head.

"Have you seen the pigeons eat this morning?"

"No."

"Maybe they haven't been fed," Timmie said.

"He always feeds them first thing," Mark answered. He studied the food containers to see if they had been filled that morning.

"I know," Timmie went on. "But maybe he ran out of food or something and had to go for more."

"He never forgets to get food," Mark responded.

I nodded my head. Mark was right. Mr.

Faraday had lots of food in his shed, enough to feed us for several weeks.

"Something sure is wrong," said Mark. "The birds never act like that. They are upset about something." Mark cupped his chin in his hand and appeared to be thinking hard. Suddenly, his head snapped up.

"I know! Mr. Faraday is sick. That's it. It's got to be. He wouldn't let anything else stop him from caring for his pigeons."

"Come on," Timmie said, grabbing Mark's sleeve. "We'd better get over there and see what's wrong."

When the boys reached the door, Timmie stepped slightly behind his older brother. His eyes were dark with fright. Mark took a deep breath, stretched his neck to try to see in the window, then knocked lightly on the door.

Even from where I was sitting I could

tell Mr. Faraday was not coming to the door.

"Maybe he can't get up," said Mark.

Timmie's eyes filled with horror. "You think he's *that* sick?"

"Might be. If he hasn't fed his pigeons, he's pretty sick all right."

"What do we do now?" asked Timmie.

"He's got a stepladder somewhere. I've seen him use it. We'll put it to the window."

Both boys bounded off the porch and went in search of Mr. Faraday's ladder. They found it hanging on the side of his grain shed. It took both of them to carry the ladder and position it beneath a window. As Timmie steadied it, Mark climbed up to peer in the window.

"Can you see anything?" whispered Timmie, worry in his voice.

"It's him!" Mark yelled. "He's on the floor."

CHAPTER
Five

Whated next was confusing. The boys ran home to call an ambulance. Then they came back with their mother to help the doctors find Mr. Faraday. All the while, our entire flock waited nervously.

Once the ambulance had left, its siren screaming down the road, Mark and Timmie came around to our loft. I watched them with a nervous eye. I knew they were nice, but what if they tried to take us while Mr. Faraday was gone? What were they going to do?

Mark hesitated, then looked around. Seeing Mr. Faraday's hose on the ground, he used it to fill up our water dish.

"What's he doing?" grumbled a pigeon.

"Looks like he's putting some water in our dish," I said in a soft whisper.

"That's Faraday's job!" a bird yelled.

"He shouldn't be doing that," said another. "I'll bet he doesn't even know how to fill it right."

"Just the same," I said. "It sure would be nice to have a drink."

"He might poison us," cried a bird, cocking her head and looking distrustfully at the boy.

"Why would he want to do that?" I answered.

The flock watched as Mark rinsed the water dish with the water from the hose and carefully refilled it. Then he ran to turn off the hose and wound it back up on its reel. After he had finished, he backed away and sat down under the shade tree that grew beside the yellow house. This was the very spot where Mr. Faraday sat after he had fed and watered the birds. As soon as the man took this position, the flock would leave the roof and dip to the ground to feed and water.

I could stand it no longer. With a light spring into the air, I stretched my wings and drifted down to the offered water. I sure was thirsty. The water felt so good as it trickled down my throat. I dipped my beak in again and swallowed some more.

By the time I was taking my third swallow,

some of the other pigeons had joined me. They, too, were thirstily drinking from the water dish.

Very carefully, I snuck a peek at Mark and saw a warm smile light his face. There was something so nice about the smile. It made me feel happy. After all, our whole flock knew that Mr. Faraday loved us, but he was not one to smile.

Six

Mark and Timmie were smart enough to find a sack of leftover grain. They did a great job feeding us. Of course, we were so hungry, anything would have tasted good!

"We need to find out how to care for these birds while Mr. Faraday is in the hospital," Mark said.

I was glad he'd thought of that. If Mr. Faraday wasn't going to be back home for a while, someone needed to care for us.

"I bet Mom will want to visit Mr.

Faraday sometime today, to check on him. Why don't we ask her if we can go along. That way, we can offer to feed his birds for him. Maybe he'll be able to give us a key to his storage shed."

Excellent idea, Mark! I thought to myself. Other birds in the flock flapped their wings in agreement. We were glad there was still someone to look out for us.

Later that afternoon, Mark approached our loft with a large birdcage. He opened it up and set it on the ground. Then he spoke.

"We're going to go see Mr. Faraday. I know he'd be real excited if one of you came along. Will one of you come with us?" Mark looked at all of us with a hopeful expression.

I knew right away what I had to do. Without a word to the others, I swooped down to the ground and walked right into that cage. Mark was surprised that I had responded so quickly. But he was right. Mr. Faraday would feel better if he could see one of us.

Mark carefully carried me, cage and all, to their car. It was a bumpy, noisy ride. But before long, we were pulling into the hospital parking lot.

The hospital was a big building. It was made of brick, and it stretched out in every direction. I had flown over it many times, but I'd never been inside it. Would they let me in? Would Mr. Faraday, grouchy as he was, let Mark and Timmie take care of us? And if not, then who would?

CHAPTER
Seven

S omehow Mr. Faraday looked smaller than I had remembered him. There was not a scowl on his face, either. Just a very worried look. His eyes brightened when he saw the boys carrying me. He stretched out a weak hand to stroke my wing through the sides of the cage.

There was a doctor with Mr. Faraday. He said something about Mr. Faraday's having had a "stroke." He would be all right, but he needed to stay in the hospital for two weeks.

"Mr. Faraday is having a bit of trouble talking right now," explained the doctor. "I'm sure he'll want to talk with you, though. He can write you messages on this paper." He pulled a pad and a pencil from his pocket and took Mr. Faraday's hand.

Mark and Timmie's mom pulled the doctor aside and spoke with him in hushed whispers. Mark and Timmie had pressed their backs against the wall, afraid to get too close to Mr. Faraday. But Mr. Faraday was glad to see them. I could tell. I could see the relief on his face that we had come.

"Mr. Faraday, these two boys are willing to take care of your pigeons until you are feeling well again," explained the doctor. "They've come to get instructions from you so they can care for them just as you would if you were able."

I didn't know if I just imagined it, or if I actually saw tears in Mr. Faraday's eyes.

It took Mr. Faraday a long time to care-fully write down the instructions about the

basic care of the flock. He looked at each boy before we left. Sure as the wings on my back, he had a smile on his face.

Mark and Timmie told him to get well soon, and I cooed my own warm wishes, as well. Mr. Faraday waved good-bye, and we were on our way.

In his small hand, Timmie clutched the carefully penciled notes, the key to Mr. Faraday's house, and the directions for where to find the key to the feed shed.

I couldn't wait to get back to the loft to tell all the others we were going to be all right.

CHAPTER
Eight

I could hear the other pigeons murmuring as Mark carried me back to the loft. They quieted down when they saw Mark and Timmie, though. Even though they knew the boys' faces, no one knew if they could trust them.

After Mark and Timmie left to go into Mr. Faraday's house, the other birds jumped on me with their questions.

"What happened?"

"How is Faraday?"

"When will he be home?"

"What's going to happen?"

I silenced everyone by flapping my wings. Then I tried to tell them everything that had happened.

"Mr. Faraday is going to be all right, but he needs to stay in the hospital for a while. Mark and Timmie are very nice. We don't have to be afraid of them. They took good care of me, and they got all the right instructions for our care from Faraday. They're going to do all the work while Faraday is gone."

"What?" screeched another bird. "How can Faraday trust anyone but himself to take care of us? We're homing pigeons, you know. We need special care."

"Listen to me. Faraday can't do it. But I promise, Mark and Timmie will take care of us. Faraday told them everything they need to know. They won't make a mistake. They want to help. They're not here to hurt us. They're here to make sure we get the proper care."

As I finished my words, the back door slammed. Mark and Timmie were headed for the feed shed. All our eyes watched the two boys. Everyone wanted to know if they would get the system right. Our survival was at stake.

Mark and Timmie were oblivious to our eyes on them. I couldn't help but notice how excited they were to be able to take care of us. Finally, even though they could have no pets of their own, they had the chance to take care of us. They had never been happier.

CHAPTER
Nine

Mr. Faraday had given the boys perfect instructions. While we birds waited, Mark and Timmie spread the pieces of paper on the ground in front of them. The two boys carefully worked through the instructions that Mr. Faraday had written.

"We need to hurry before the pigeons get hungry for dinner," said Mark. "And we need to be real quiet and gentle. They might still be scared."

Taking their instructions with them, they went inside the feed shed and identified the different seeds and grains. They picked up the different measuring scoops, organized the bags of food, and even swept the floor. I knew Mr. Faraday would have been pleased.

When they had the feed mixed just right, they placed it in the pigeon food containers. They locked the shed door so no one else could come in. Then they carefully hung the key back on the hook by the kitchen cupboards. They even put fresh water in the water dish.

Much to our surprise, Mark and Timmie headed home. We saw them after a minute or two. Both boys' heads peeked up from their side of the fence. They were keeping their distance, wanting to give us some privacy for dinner.

I gave the rest of the flock a look that said, "I told you so." Then I swooped down to our meal. It was perfect! Just the way Mr. Faraday mixed it up. The other birds, after taking a couple of bites, agreed with me.

Mark and Timmie cheered at the sight of us eating. I flew up to perch on the fence near their heads. Their eyes twinkled with delight. Anyone could see they were true animal lovers. Too bad Mr. Faraday wouldn't let them have pets. Mark and Timmie would be the best caretakers around.

Edging just a bit closer, I cooed my thanks to them for a job well done.

"Do you think he's saying thank you?" asked Timmie with a gasp.

"Sure looks like it to me," Mark answered. "They're really smart birds."

I puffed my chest out with pride.

"Mr. Faraday sure is lucky to have so many nice birds," Timmie said with a dreamy look on his face.

And Mr. Faraday sure is lucky to have such great neighbors like you, I thought to myself.

CHAPTER
Ten

The days went by quickly. Mark and Timmie came every morning and every evening to feed us and give us water. They also came on Saturday morning to clean out our lofts. I don't think Mr. Faraday had asked them to do that. But that just shows what wonderful boys they were.

Mark always greeted us with a big smile. And Timmie used his softest voice to talk to us as they worked. By now, the entire flock trusted the boys completely.

I missed Mr. Faraday. But something else was happening in me that took me by surprise. I found myself looking forward to our feeding times now more than ever. Not just because it was time to eat. No, it was more than that. I was becoming good friends with the boys, and my favorite times in the day were when they were in our yard.

Mark and Timmie couldn't get enough of me. They brought books about pigeons to read as they sat in the grass. And Timmie would watch me eat, making sure I had enough food. They both boasted that I could easily fly farther than all the other pigeons. I think I was becoming their favorite.

And I, in turn, eagerly tried to get their approval by doing little tricks for them. For instance, I could fly up to the branches of the trees and hide. Then I would swoop back down to my loft when they called.

I tried not to worry about the fact that Mr. Faraday would be home any day now. I supposed he would turn into his grumpy old self again. And while I knew he would take excellent care of all us birds, I didn't think he would let Mark and Timmie into his yard again.

Mark and Timmie probably thought so, too, for during the last few days they spent every waking moment with us. It was sad. We tried to enjoy our time together, because all too soon it was going to come to an end.

CHAPTER
Eleven

Finally the day we had all been waiting for came. Mr. Faraday was coming home. All the birds were excited, even me. We loved Mark and Timmie, but we also had a special place in our hearts for the man who had raised us and cared for us all these years. The big question on everyone's mind, though, was what would happen to Mark and Timmie.

Mr. Faraday had only been home a few minutes before he was walking out the back door, greeting all of us. We welcomed him by cooing excitedly.

He used a cane to get around, and he looked pretty wobbly. But the expression of pure joy on his face meant he was happy to be home.

For a few days, Mark and Timmie stayed on their side of the fence. They watched us closely when Mr. Faraday wasn't around. But as soon as Mr. Faraday came outside, the boys ran into their house as quickly as they could. How I missed Mark and Timmie's gentle hands and happy spirit.

I was really curious now. What would Mr. Faraday do now that he was home? And then one morning, it all became clear.

Mr. Faraday was sweeping out the feed shed. He was moving pretty slow, but he was doing a fine job on his own. Mark and Timmie were playing in their backyard, and

Mr. Faraday heard them. With a twinkle in his eye, Mr. Faraday glanced at the fence, put down his broom, and let out a low moan.

"Ooooowww," he cried.

Mark and Timmie both ran to the fence.

"Are you okay, Mr. Faraday? Can we help you?" Mark asked.

"Well," said Faraday. "I am having a hard time with this broom. Suppose you boys were to come over and help me. Would you want to do that?"

"You bet!" came the happy cry, and within minutes Mark and Timmie were at his side, helping him sit so they could take over.

"Well, what do you know," I muttered under my breath. "It looks like ol' Faraday has a changed heart after all."

CHAPTER
Twelve

The summer wore on. And even after Mr. Faraday began to hobble about without his cane, he still seemed to expect the boys' daily visit. Gone was the grouchy neighbor they had known when they first moved into the rented house. Instead, Mr. Faraday seemed to enjoy the company of the two young boys almost as much as he enjoyed their helping hands.

I was so happy. Not only was Mr. Faraday a much happier man, I still got to spend time with Mark and Timmie. They took turns working with me, following the training lessons Mr. Faraday was giving. I could tell they were both naturals. Their love of animals sure helped, but deep down in their hearts, I could tell they had a special love for us pigeons.

Mr. Faraday spent much of his time sitting on the porch and watching us birds and the boys. On occasion, he would tell old stories about his pigeons while Mark and Timmie listened intently. Pigeons were their new delight, and the talk of pigeons was absolutely interesting. Mr. Faraday assured them they would grow up to be great trainers.

"Yeah," Timmie agreed. "It will be super when we get a bird of our own." His eyes gazed dreamily at me.

Mr. Faraday was a changed man now, and as he and the boys sat upon the porch sipping lemonade that Mark's mom had made, he surprised them with an exciting suggestion.

CHAPTER
Thirteen

Mr. Faraday looked shy all of a sudden. He cleared his throat, then he began.

"I've watched you fellas work with the birds for some time now, and it seems to me that you are first-rate. It's about time you had a loft of your own."

"We could never afford one," Mark said. "It's all Mom can do to pay the rent and buy the groceries."

"Yeah," agreed Timmie. "Good birds cost lots of money—and I wouldn't want just any old birds."

A twinkle showed in Mr. Faraday's eyes. "You like good birds, huh?" he grunted.

"Yeah," said both boys at once.

"You think I have good birds?" continued Mr. Faraday.

I puffed out my chest. Of course! We were the best!

"Yeah," said the boys. "The best."

"Well, I agree with you on that one," chuckled Mr. Faraday. "Now, if I was to tell you that you can pick a bird—any one from the loft—which one would you pick?"

The boys thought that Mr. Faraday was playing a little game with them.

"That's easy," said Mark. "I'd pick Blue Boy."

It was hard to puff my chest out any farther than I already had, but after hearing that, I tried.

"And you?" asked Mr. Faraday, turning to Timmie.

"I would, too," said Timmie. "He's the

prettiest, and the fastest—and I think he's the smartest, too."

"You do, eh?" said Mr. Faraday with another chuckle. "Well, you're even smarter than I thought. You are right, and I'd pick Blue Boy, too." Then Mr. Faraday laughed out loud. "You little rascals," he said. "You just beat me out of my best bird."

I felt my beak drop open. Did I hear right? The boys just looked at the old man.

"So how do you plan to care for your pigeon?" said Mr. Faraday. "You need a loft, you know."

"What do you mean?" asked Timmie innocently.

"I mean, I'm giving you Blue Boy."

"But...but..."

"No buts, he's yours now."

Timmie threw his arms around Mr. Faraday's neck, the tears streaming down his face. Mark followed the lead of his younger brother.

Mr. Faraday wiped away a few tears of his own as he watched the two boys run excitedly home, hardly able to believe their good news. Mrs. Thomas could hear them coming long before they ever reached the back door.

"We've got a pigeon! We've got a pigeon! Our very own! Our very own pigeon!"

CHAPTER
Fourteen

In the warm summer days that followed, and under the careful eye of Mr. Faraday, the loft was built. It was great fun. And never had I seen Mark, Timmie, or Mr. Faraday happier.

Mr. Faraday was now a good friend. To the boys, he was almost a grandfather.

"You know," said Mark one morning. "The loft looks so bare. Mr. Faraday's is a nice blue-gray color. Ours should be painted, too. Let's paint it. We can paint the loft a whole bunch of nice colors."

Right away, the boys set to work. I watched, too. I couldn't wait to see what my new home was going to look like. All afternoon they painted—coloring one section a bright orange, another section green, then one blue. They added bits of pink to the peak, some chocolate brown to some perches, and trimmed it with yellow.

"It looks great," said Timmie. "Mom will like it, too. Bet there's no other loft anywhere as pretty or as colorful as ours."

Their loft was colorful, all right. Some folks might have questioned the "pretty" part, yet the two boys beamed with pride.

"Did you know that in some places, they call lofts 'cotes'?" Mark said to Timmie.

Timmie looked up in surprise. "I thought cotes were for sheep," he said.

"That's right—sheep or pigeons. They call both of them cotes."

"Why don't we call our loft a cote?" asked Timmie.

"'Cause here in our country, they call

them lofts."

"That doesn't mean *we* have to," insisted Timmie. "We painted ours different. We can call it different, too, if we want to."

To Mark it made perfect sense. "Let's," he said. "Mr. Faraday's will be the *loft*. Ours will be the *cote*. Then we will never get mixed up about which one we are talking about."

I heard their mother chuckle. Mark and Timmie turned around, and we all looked at her, wondering what was funny.

"I was just thinking," she said with the laugh that was bubbling up within her. "Your cote—it's a cote of many colors."

The two boys joined in her laughter.

CHAPTER
Fifteen

Well, that's my story. Who would have thought that a little bird like me could change so many lives? You know, there are a lot of people out there that don't like pigeons. They think all we do is live in parks and get in the way. Well, the next time you run into people like that, you can tell them my story. I bet that would change their minds!

I really love living in my colorful cote at Mark and Timmie's house. I still see my pigeon friends every day. After all, we're only a few feet away from each other.

Mr. Faraday is all better these days. He can move about really well, and doesn't need help with anything. Of course, that doesn't stop Mark and Timmie from visiting him every day. Just think, if Mr. Faraday had never gotten sick, then Mark and Timmie would still be without a pet. And Mr. Faraday would still be without two great friends. It's great to see all things work together for good.

BETHANY BACKYARD®

PICTURE BOOKS

Spunky's First Christmas
by Janette Oke

Spunky's Camping Adventure
by Janette Oke

Spunky's Circus Adventure
by Janette Oke

Annie Ashcraft Looks Into the Dark
by Ruth Senter

Cows in the House
by Beverly Lewis

*Princess Bella and the
Red Velvet Hat*
by T. Davis Bunn

Making Memories
by Janette Oke

Hold the Boat!
by Jeremiah Gamble

Annika's Secret Wish
by Beverly Lewis

Fifteen Flamingos
by Elspeth Campbell Murphy

Sanji's Seed
by B. J. Reinhard

Happy Easter, God!
by Elspeth Campbell Murphy

BOARD BOOKS by Christine Tangvald

God Made Colors...For Me!
God Made Shapes...For Me!

God's 123s...For Me!
God's ABCs...For Me!

REBUS PICTURE BOOKS by Christine Tangvald

The Bible Is...For Me!
Christmas Is...For Me!
Easter Is...For Me!

Jesus Is...For Me!
Prayer Is...For Me!
God Is...For Me!

FIRST CHAPTER BOOKS by Janette Oke

Spunky's Diary
The Prodigal Cat
The Impatient Turtle
This Little Pig
New Kid in Town
Ducktails

Prairie Dog Town
Trouble in a Fur Coat
Maury Had a Little Lamb
Pordy's Prickly Problem
A Cote of Many Colors
Who's New at the Zoo?

NONFICTION

*Glow-in-the-Dark Fish and
59 More Ways to See God
Through His Creation*

*Our Place in Space and
59 More Ways to See God
Through His Creation*
by B. J. Reinhard

*The Wonderful Way Babies
Are Made*
by Larry Christenson

Fins, Feathers, and Faith
by William L. Coleman

Series for Young Readers*
From Bethany House Publishers

THE ADVENTURES OF CALLIE ANN
by Shannon Mason Leppard

Readers will giggle their way through the true-to-life escapades of Callie Ann Davies and her many North Carolina friends.

ASTROKIDS
by Robert Elmer

Space scooters? Floating robots? Jupiter ice cream? Blast into the future for out-of-this-world, zero-gravity fun with the AstroKids on space station *CLEO-7*.

BACKPACK MYSTERIES
by Mary Carpenter Reid

This excitement-filled mystery series follows the mishaps and adventures of Steff and Paulie Larson as they strive to help often-eccentric relatives crack their toughest cases.

THE CUL-DE-SAC KIDS
by Beverly Lewis

Each story in this lighthearted series features the hilarious antics and predicaments of nine endearing boys and girls who live on Blossom Hill Lane.

JANETTE OKE'S ANIMAL FRIENDS
by Janette Oke

Endearing creatures from the farm, forest, and zoo discover their place in God's world through various struggles, mishaps, and adventures.

THREE COUSINS DETECTIVE CLUB®
by Elspeth Campbell Murphy

Famous detective cousins Timothy, Titus, and Sarah-Jane learn compelling Scripture-based truths while finding—and solving—intriguing mysteries.